Geronimo Stilton
ENGLISH!

22 A FUN DAY 好玩的一天

U0061307

新雅文化事業有限公司
www.sunya.com.hk

Geronimo Stilton English
A FUN DAY 好玩的一天

作　　者：Geronimo Stilton 謝利連摩·史提頓
譯　　者：申倩
責任編輯：王燕參
封面繪圖：Giuseppe Facciotto
插圖繪畫：Claudio Cernuschi, Andrea Denegri, Daria Cerchi
內文設計：Angela Ficarelli, Raffaella Picozzi
出　　版：新雅文化事業有限公司
　　　　　香港英皇道499號北角工業大廈18樓
　　　　　電話：（852）2138 7998
　　　　　傳真：（852）2597 4003
　　　　　網址：http://www.sunya.com.hk
　　　　　電郵：marketing@sunya.com.hk
發　　行：香港聯合書刊物流有限公司
　　　　　香港新界大埔汀麗路36號中華商務印刷大廈3字樓
　　　　　電話：（852）2150 2100　傳真：（852）2407 3062
　　　　　電郵：info@suplogistics.com.hk
印　　刷：C & C Offset Printing Co.,Ltd
　　　　　香港新界大埔汀麗路36號
版　　次：二〇一二年七月初版
　　　　　10 9 8 7 6 5 4 3 2 1

ISBN: 978-962-08-5549-8
© 2008 Edizioni Piemme S.p.A., Via Tiziano 32 - 20145 Milano - Italia
International Rights © 2007 Atlantyca S.p.A. - via Leopardi, 8, Milano - Italy
© 2012 for this Work in Traditional Chinese language, Sun Ya Publications (HK) Ltd.
18/F, North Point Industrial Building, 499 King's Road, Hong Kong.
Published and printed in Hong Kong

CONTENTS
目錄

BENJAMIN'S CLASSMATES
班哲文的老師和同學們

Maestra Topitilla
托比蒂拉·德·托比莉斯

Rarin
拉琳

Diego
迪哥

Rupa
露芭

Tui
杜爾

David
大衛

Sakura
櫻花

Mohamed
穆哈麥德

Tian Kai
田凱

Oliver
奧利佛

Milenko
米蘭哥

Trippo
特里普

Carmen
卡敏

Atina
阿提娜

Esmeralda
愛絲梅拉達

Pandora
潘朵拉

Takeshi
北野

Kuti
菊花

Benjamin
班哲文

Hsing
阿星

Laura
羅拉

Kiku
奇哥

Antonia
安東妮婭

Liza
麗莎

GERONIMO AND HIS FRIENDS

謝利連摩和他的家鼠朋友們

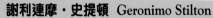

謝利連摩・史提頓 Geronimo Stilton
一個古怪的傢伙，簡直可以說是一隻笨拙的文化鼠。他是
《鼠民公報》的總裁，正花盡心思改變報紙業的歷史。

菲・史提頓 Tea Stilton
謝利連摩的妹妹，她是《鼠民公報》的特派記者，同
時也是一個運動愛好者。

班哲文・史提頓 Benjamin Stilton
謝利連摩的小侄兒，常被叔叔稱作「我的
小乳酪」，是一隻感情豐富的小老鼠。

潘朵拉・華之鼠 Pandora Woz
柏蒂・活力鼠的姨甥女、班哲文最好的朋友，
是一隻活潑開朗的小老鼠。

柏蒂・活力鼠 Patty Spring
美麗迷人的電視新聞工作者，致力於她熱愛的電視事業。

賴皮 Trappola
謝利連摩的表弟，非常喜歡食物，風趣幽默，是一隻饞
嘴、愛開玩笑的老鼠，善於將歡樂傳遞給每一隻鼠。

麗萍姑媽 Zia Lippa
謝利連摩的姑媽，對鼠十分友善，又和藹可親，只想將
最好的給身邊的鼠。

艾拿 Iena
謝利連摩的好朋友，充滿活力，熱愛各項運動，他希望
能把對運動的熱誠傳給謝利連摩。

史奎克・愛管閒事鼠 Ficcanaso Squitt
謝利連摩的好朋友，是一個非常有頭腦的私家
偵探，總是穿着一件黃色的乾濕褸。

A FUN DAY　好玩的一天

　　親愛的小朋友，今天我要去遊樂場玩，本來我不是很想去，是我的小侄兒班哲文說服我一起去的，他說那裏好玩極了，而且我們的朋友也去。可是，一想到要坐過山車，我就緊張得臉色發青，我以一千塊莫澤雷勒乳酪發誓，就像我身上的綠色外套一樣青！還有，一想到去鬼屋，我就全身汗毛豎起！嗯，求求你們，和我一起去好嗎？也許這樣我能稍稍安心一點！

跟我謝利連摩・史提頓一起學英文，
就像玩遊戲一樣簡單好玩！

你可以一邊看着圖畫一邊讀。
以下有幾個標誌，你要特別留意：

當看到 💿 標誌時，你可以聽CD，
一邊聽，一邊跟着朗讀，還可以跟
着一起唱歌。

當看到 ⭐ 標誌時，你可以和朋友
們一起玩遊戲，或者嘗試回答問
題。題目很簡單，它們對鞏固你所
學過的內容很有幫助。

當看到 ❗ 標誌時，你要注意看一
下格子裏的生字，反覆唸幾遍，掌
握發音。

最後，不要忘記完成小測驗和練習
冊裏的問題！看看你有多聰明吧。

祝大家學得開開心心！

謝利連摩・史提頓

AT THE FUNFAIR
在遊樂場裏

一走進遊樂場，班哲文和潘朵拉就急不及待拉着我去坐摩天輪，我們坐在摩天輪上欣賞遊樂場的全景，遊樂場裏的設施真多呢！你也跟着班哲文和潘朵拉一起學習這些設施的英文名稱吧！

pirate ship

musical train

ticket office

haunted house

⭐ 1. 試着用英語説出：
摩天輪、過山車。

A SONG FOR YOU!
Track 1

Let's Go to the Funfair
I'm going to the funfair to play and ride the roller coaster all day. Do you want to come with me? It's great fun, come along and see!

8

roller coaster

big wheel

chairoplane

hall of mirrors

merry-go-round

racing cars

dodgems

9

THE BIG WHEEL 摩天輪

在摩天輪上，我們可以看到整個老鼠島的景色，真是美麗極了！但是，我以一千塊莫澤雷勒乳酪發誓，沒有人記得照顧我……我因為畏高而正全身發抖得很厲害呢！

剛從摩天輪下來，班哲文和潘朵拉就跑去小食亭買棉花糖了。

neither 也不
too 也是

We are enjoying ourselves on the big wheel!

Yes, we're having lots of fun!

I'm afraid of heights, I'm not enjoying myself!

Neither am I.

I would like some candyfloss!

We would, too!

⭐ 試用英語說出以下的句子：

1. 我們在摩天輪上很開心！

2. 我有畏高症。

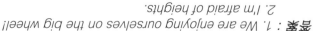

FROM 60 TO 100!
由60數到100！

我的臉色仍蒼白得像塊莫澤雷勒乳酪，為了分散我的注意力，潘朵拉帶我去玩夾波子。這個遊戲真好玩，同時可以學習數數。你也跟着我們一起數吧！

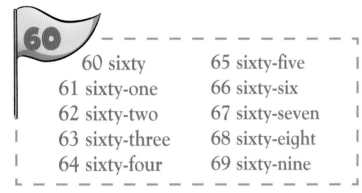

60

60 sixty	65 sixty-five
61 sixty-one	66 sixty-six
62 sixty-two	67 sixty-seven
63 sixty-three	68 sixty-eight
64 sixty-four	69 sixty-nine

70

70 seventy	75 seventy-five
71 seventy-one	76 seventy-six
72 seventy-two	77 seventy-seven
73 seventy-three	78 seventy-eight
74 seventy-four	79 seventy-nine

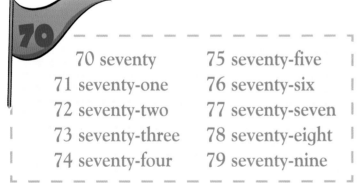

80

80 eighty	85 eighty-five
81 eighty-one	86 eighty-six
82 eighty-two	87 eighty-seven
83 eighty-three	88 eighty-eight
84 eighty-four	89 eighty-nine

90

90 ninety
91 ninety-one
92 ninety-two
93 ninety-three
94 ninety-four
95 ninety-five
96 ninety-six
97 ninety-seven
98 ninety-eight
99 ninety-nine

100

100 a hundred/one hundred

⭐ 試用英語説出：60, 70, 80, 90, 100, 61, 73, 81, 83, 95, 97。

答案：sixty, seventy, eighty, ninety, a hundred / one hundred, sixty-one, seventy-three, eighty-one, eighty-three, ninety-five, ninety-seven

THE PIRATE SHIP　海盜船

班哲文和潘朵拉看到海盜船前排隊的人少了些，
就趕快跑過去排隊。

If we lose sight of each other, we'll meet here, at the candyfloss stall.

Wait, kids! Don't run!

❗ if　如果

Pandora always enjoys herself very much on the pirate ship!

I want to go on the pirate ship!

Me, too!

So does Benjamin!

 ⭐ 試着用英語説出：「不要跑！」

12

我在一張長椅上坐下來，我為自己感到疲累而覺得有點不好意思……我不想讓別人知道我的體質如此弱！這時柏蒂走過來坐在我身邊，連艾拿和菲也來了……不知道他們是真的累了，還是特意過來陪我的！

> So am I.
> 我也是。

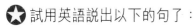

⭐ 試用英語説出以下的句子：

1. 我口渴了。我也是。

2. 我不餓。我也不。

THE MERRY-GO-ROUND
旋轉木馬

玩完海盜船之後，班哲文和潘朵拉想放鬆一下，玩一些比較靜態的遊戲，於是他們去玩旋轉木馬！

merry-go-round

spaceship

dragon

carriage

horse

Pandora is enjoying herself very much on the merry-go-round.

Benjamin is enjoying himself, too.

Geronimo is relaxed: the merry-go-round moves slowly, there are no dangers!

史奎克也想去玩旋轉木馬，但菲跟他說要等下一輪才可以玩！

艾拿想在力量測試中挑戰賴皮，還在賴皮面前展示他的肌肉……賴皮知道他的力量不及艾拿，他還是比較擅長開玩笑。

wait for 等候

telling jokes 講笑話

15

THE HAUNTED HOUSE 鬼屋

我的心情還沒完全平伏下來，現在只想好好休息一會兒，但艾拿卻堅持要去鬼屋看看，我只好跟着一起進去。大家都玩得開心極了，可是我的臉色卻又蒼白得像塊莫澤雷勒乳酪。

scared 害怕

Everybody is having great fun in the haunted house except for Geronimo: he's scared of the dark, of ghosts, of spiders.

THE HALL OF MIRRORS
鏡屋

終於來到柏蒂最喜歡的地方——鏡屋了。看到鏡子中自己變了形的樣子，多好玩啊！不過要注意，在鏡屋裏要把手爪舉起來，不然你的鼻子很容易會撞到鏡子上去！

試用英語說出以下的句子：

1. 你好高！
2. 我比你高！
3. 我最高！

答案：1. You are so tall! 2. I'm taller than you! 3. I'm the tallest!

17

FIREWORKS 煙花表演

今天的節目真豐富啊，但還欠最後一樣——一場煙花表演！七彩繽紛的顏色，千變萬化的形狀，實在太漂亮了！可惜很快就到了回家的時間，班哲文和潘朵拉多希望這一天永遠不要結束啊！

a lot of 很多

A SONG FOR YOU! Track 2

At the Funfair

When I go to the funfair
I go on the merry-go-round
I go on the pirate ship
and I have great fun!
The funfair is fantastic
I buy some balloons
I eat some candyfloss
and I have great fun!
I go on the big wheel
I throw rings
I go on the chairoplane
and I have great fun!
The funfair is fantastic
I buy some balloons
I eat some candyfloss
and I have great fun!

They are beautiful! I would like to stay and watch them.

Oh, yes, me too!

試用英語説出以下的句子：
1. 你們玩得開心嗎？
2. 我們玩得開心極了！

答案：1. Did you enjoy yourselves?
2. We enjoyed ourselves very much!

19

〈遊樂場捉賊記〉

謝利連摩：我的手提箱！有鼠偷去了我的手提箱！

潘朵拉：裏面有些什麼東西？

菲：他那本新書的稿件。但是……誰會偷這些東西？

遊客甲：我看見一隻男鼠拿着一個手提箱！他的個子很高！
遊客乙：不，他的個子很矮！

史奎克：我們問問附近的遊客有沒有見過吧。

遊客丙：他很苗條！
遊客丁：不，他很健壯！
謝利連摩：但是……你們在哪裏見過他？

班哲文：這很明顯，叔叔……

班哲文：在鏡屋裏！
那裏每隻鼠看起來都會不一樣。

菲：這樣，我們找到的線索都沒有用！
嘿，這很有趣，對吧？

柏蒂：對，看看我！

謝利連摩：嘿，我們什麼時候去找回我的手提箱呢？

潘朵拉：不用擔心，我們一定能找回它的。

史奎克：潘朵拉，在你後面，他正向着過山車那邊跑去！

史奎克：來吧，謝利連摩！快上來！

菲：沒時間了！

謝利連摩：但是我很害怕！

菲：坐在這裏，我會握着你的手爪！

謝利連摩：好吧！

22

史奎克：那個賊和你的手提箱就在那邊！

謝利連摩：算吧，我可以把所有稿件全部給他。

史奎克：那個賊就在這裏！他看起來是不是有點面熟？
謝利連摩：我不敢相信！

謝利連摩：賴皮，你為什麼這樣做？
賴皮：只是想你坐坐過山車而已！很有趣，對吧？
謝利連摩：我的胃不認為這是一個好主意。

TEST 小測驗

⭐ 1. 讀出下面的英文詞彙，把相配的中英文詞彙用線連起來。

dodgems　　　　　●　　　　　● 鬼屋

roller coaster　　●　　　　　● 過山車

merry-go-round　●　　　　　● 碰碰車

haunted house　　●　　　　　● 旋轉木馬

⭐ 2. 讀出下面的英文句子，並用中文說出它們的意思。

I'm taller than you!

I'm shorter than you!

Pandora　　　　　　　　　　　　　　　　　Benjamin

⭐ 3. 用英語說出下面的數字。

| 75 | 77 | 82 | 84 | 89 | 91 | 96 | 99 |

⭐ 4. 用英語說出下面的句子。

(a) 我有點累。我也是！

I am … … … . … , too!

(b) 我口渴了！我也是！

I'm … ! So … … !

⭐ 5. 「那是什麼？是煙花！」用英語該怎麼說？選出正確的句子，大聲讀出來。

(a) Kids, did you enjoy yourselves? Yes, we did!

(b) What are those? They are fireworks!

DICTIONARY 詞典

（英、粵、普發聲）

A

a hundred 一百

a lot of 很多

afraid 害怕

always 經常

as long as 只要

B

balloons 氣球

beautiful 美麗

because 因為

behind 後面

believe 相信

bench 長椅

big wheel 摩天輪

book 書

C

candyfloss 棉花糖

carriage 馬車

chairoplane 飛天鞦韆

clues 線索

D

dangers 危險

dark 黑暗

different 不同

dodgems 碰碰車

dragon 龍

E

eighty 八十

except 除……之外

F

familiar 熟悉

feel 覺得

find 找到

fireworks 煙花

G

ghosts 鬼

H

hall of mirrors 鏡屋

hand 手

haunted house 鬼屋

have fun 玩得開心

heights 高度

here 這裏

herself 她自己

hold 握着

horse 馬

hungry 肚子餓

I

if 如果

K

kids 小孩

L

like 喜歡

M

meet　會合

merry-go-round　旋轉木馬

musical train　音樂火車

myself　我自己

N

next　下一個

ninety　九十

noise　噪音

O

obvious　明顯

ourselves　我們自己

over there　在那邊

P

pirate ship　海盜船

R

racing cars　小型賽車

relaxed　放鬆

ride　騎

roller coaster　過山車

run　跑

S

scared　害怕

see　看見

seventy　七十

short　矮

sit　坐

sixty　六十

slim　苗條

slowly　慢慢地

spaceship　太空船

spiders　蜘蛛

stall　攤檔

stay　停留

steal　偷

stomach　胃

suitcase　手提箱

T

tall　高

telling jokes　講笑話

thief　賊

thirsty　口渴

those　那些

throw　擲

ticket office　售票處

tired　疲倦

U

useless　沒有用

W

wait for　等候

want　想要

watch　觀看

well-built　健壯

when　什麼時候

where　哪裏

why　為什麼

worry　擔心

Y

yourselves　你們自己

看在一千塊莫澤雷勒乳酪的份上，你學得開心嗎？很開心，對不對？好極了！跟你一起跳舞唱歌我也很開心！我等着你下次繼續跟班哲文和潘朵拉一起玩一起學英語呀。現在要說再見了，當然是用英語說啦！

GERONIMO'S ISLAND
老鼠島地圖

往老鼠海峽

鯨魚出沒地

海盜貓船

海盜島

托圖加島

黑豹羣島

快樂島環礁

珊瑚礁

海豚灣

貓牙灣

臭味港

往鼠平洋

往鼠西洋

角鯊
出沒地

迷路貓港

壯鼠市

三鼠市

沙鼠城

鼠福港

老 鼠 島

拔毛島

往老鼠海

1. 大冰湖	9. 硫磺湖	17. 自然保護公園	25. 巨杉山谷	33. 鼠哈拉沙漠
2. 毛結冰山	10. 貓止步關	18. 拉斯鼠維加斯海岸	26. 梵提娜乳酪泉	34. 喘氣駱駝綠洲
3. 滑溜溜冰川	11. 醉酒峯	19. 化石森林	27. 硫磺沼澤	35. 第一山
4. 鼠皮疙瘩山	12. 黑森林	20. 小鼠湖	28. 間歇泉	36. 熱帶叢林
5. 鼠基斯坦	13. 吸血鬼谷	21. 中鼠湖	29. 田鼠谷	37. 蚊子谷
6. 鼠坦尼亞	14. 發冷山	22. 大鼠湖	30. 瘋鼠谷	
7. 吸血鬼山	15. 黑影關	23. 諾比奧拉乳酪峯	31. 蚊子沼澤	
8. 鐵板鼠火山	16. 客嗇鼠城堡	24. 肯尼貓城堡	32. 史卓奇諾乳酪城堡	

Geronimo Stilton

EXERCISE BOOK
練習冊

想知道自己對 A FUN DAY 掌握了多少，
趕快打開後面的練習完成它吧！

ENGLISH!

22 **A FUN DAY** 好玩的一天

AT THE FUNFAIR
在遊樂場裏

★ 你在遊樂場裏看到些什麼？從下面選出適當的字詞，寫在圖畫下面的橫線上。

merry-go-round　　candyfloss　　big wheel
hall of mirrors

1.

_____

2.

_____

3.

_____

4.

_____

THE BIG WHEEL　摩天輪

⭐ 他們在說什麼？從下面選出適當的句子，然後把代表答案的英文字母填在句框內。

A. I'm afraid of heights, I'm not enjoying myself!
B. I would like some candyfloss!
C. We are enjoying ourselves on the big wheel!
D. We would, too!

THE PIRATE SHIP 海盜船

★ 班哲文和潘朵拉想去哪兒玩？從下面選出適當的字詞填在橫線上，完成他們的對話，就知道了。

too   does   enjoys   pirate ship

3. Pandora always

_____

herself very much on the pirate ship!

4. So

_____

Benjamin!

1. I want to go on the

_____ ,

Benjamin!

2. Me,

_____ ,

Pandora!

THE HALL OF MIRRORS
鏡屋

⭐ 謝利連摩和朋友們來到鏡屋裏，猜猜他們在說什麼，選出適當的字詞填在橫線上，完成他們的對話。

very	short	tall

1. Pandora, you are so _____ !

2. And you are so _____ !

3. Look, I'm _____ short!

4.  Geronimo, I'm _____ than you!

5.  But in the mirror you're _____ than me!

6. I'm the _____ !

THE MERRY-GO-ROUND
旋轉木馬

⭐ 謝利連摩和孩子們坐上不同款式的旋轉木馬，玩得多開心啊！根據圖畫，從下面選出適當的字詞寫在橫線上。

horse　　carriage　　spaceship　　dragon

2. _____

3. _____

1. _____

4. _____

FIREWORKS 煙花表演

⭐ 謝利連摩和朋友們在看煙花，猜猜他們在説什麼，從下面選出適當的字詞填在橫線上，完成他們的對話。

> like　　fireworks　　a lot of　　those　　me too

1. Look, what are _____?

2. They are _____!

3. They are beautiful! I would _____ to stay and watch them.

4. Oh, yes, _____!

5. They make _____ noise.

ANSWERS 答案

TEST 小測驗

1. dodgems — 碰碰車
   roller coaster — 過山車
   merry-go-round — 旋轉木馬
   haunted house — 鬼屋

2. Pandora: 我比你高！   Benjamin: 我比你矮！

3. 75 seventy-five, 77 seventy-seven, 82 eighty-two, 84 eighty-four, 89 eighty-nine, 91 ninety-one, 96 ninety-six, 99 ninety-nine

4. (a) I am <u>a bit tired</u>. <u>Me</u>, too!
   (b) I'm <u>thirsty</u>! So <u>am I</u>!

5. (b) What are those? They are fireworks!

EXERCISE BOOK 練習冊

P.1
1. big wheel   2. candyfloss   3. hall of mirrors   4. merry-go-round

P.2
1. C   2. A   3. B   4. D

P.3
1. pirate ship   2. too   3. enjoys   4. does

P.4-5
1. short   2. tall   3. very   4. taller   5. shorter   6. tallest

P.6
1. dragon   2. carriage   3. horse   4. spaceship

P.7
1. those   2. fireworks   3. like   4. me too   5. a lot of